Swimmy

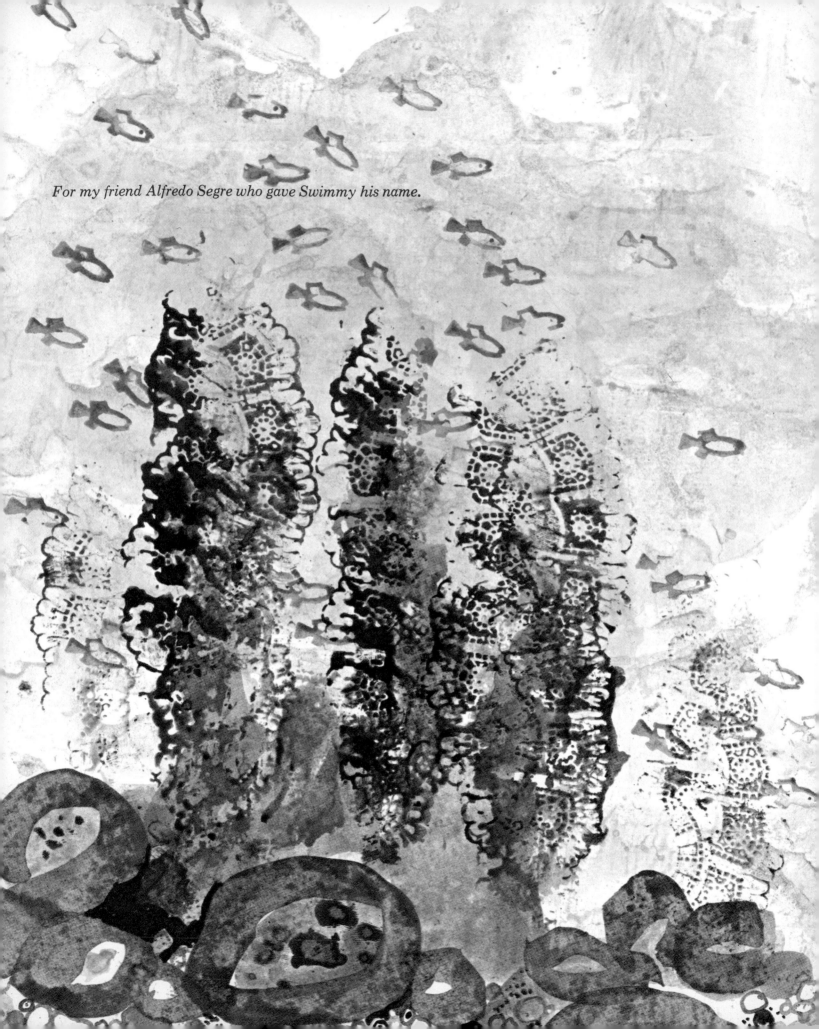

For my friend Alfredo Segre who gave Swimmy his name.

Swimmy

by Leo Lionni

 Alfred A. Knopf, New York

A happy school of little fish lived in a corner of the sea somewhere.
They were all red. Only one of them was as black as a mussel shell.
He swam faster than his brothers and sisters. His name was Swimmy.

One bad day a tuna fish, swift, fierce and very hungry, came darting
through the waves. In one gulp he swallowed all the little red fish.
Only Swimmy escaped.

He swam away in the deep wet world. He was scared, lonely and very sad.

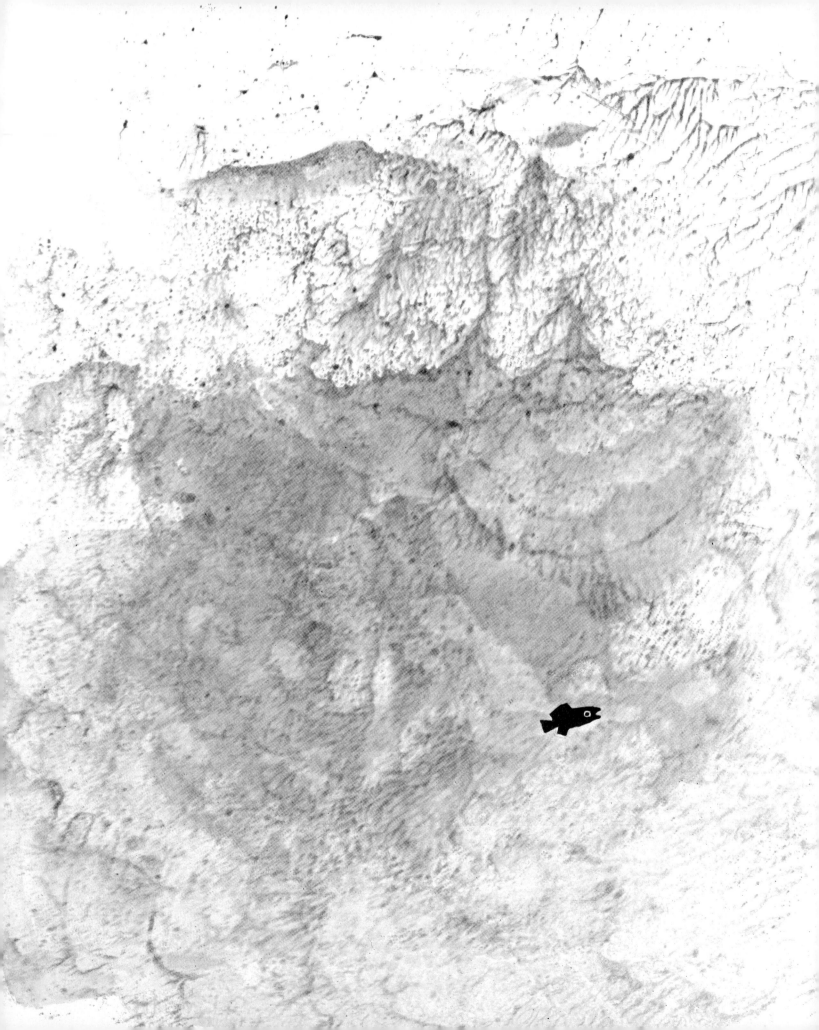

But the sea was full of wonderful creatures, and as he swam from marvel
to marvel Swimmy was happy again.

He saw a medusa made of rainbow jelly...

a lobster, who walked about like a water-moving machine...

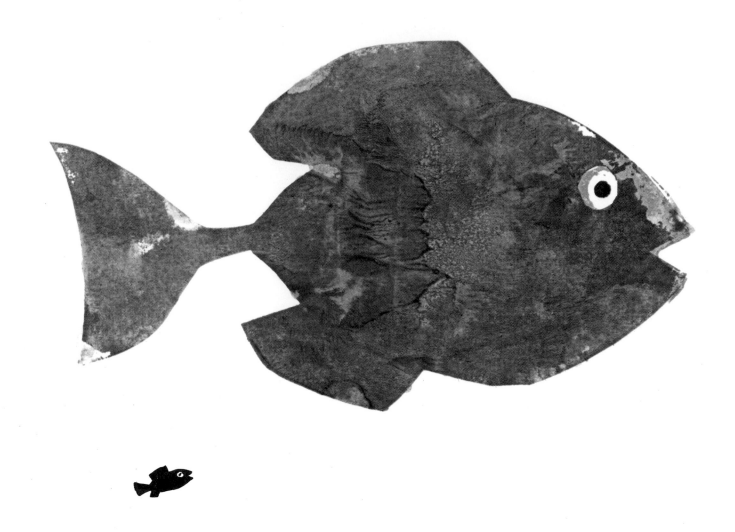

strange fish, pulled by an invisible thread...

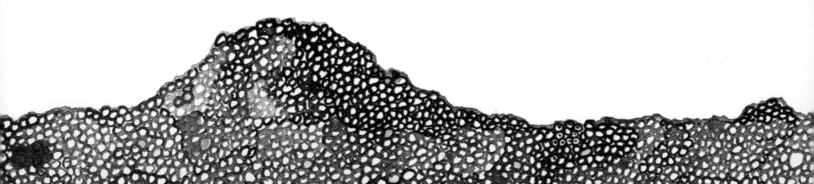

a forest of seaweeds growing from sugar-candy rocks...

an eel whose tail was almost too far away to remember...

and sea anemones, who looked like pink palm trees swaying in the wind.

Then, hidden in the dark shade of rocks and weeds, he saw a school of little fish, just like his own.

"Let's go and swim and play and SEE things!" he said happily.
"We can't," said the little red fish. "The big fish will eat us all."

"But you can't just lie there," said Swimmy. "We must THINK of something."

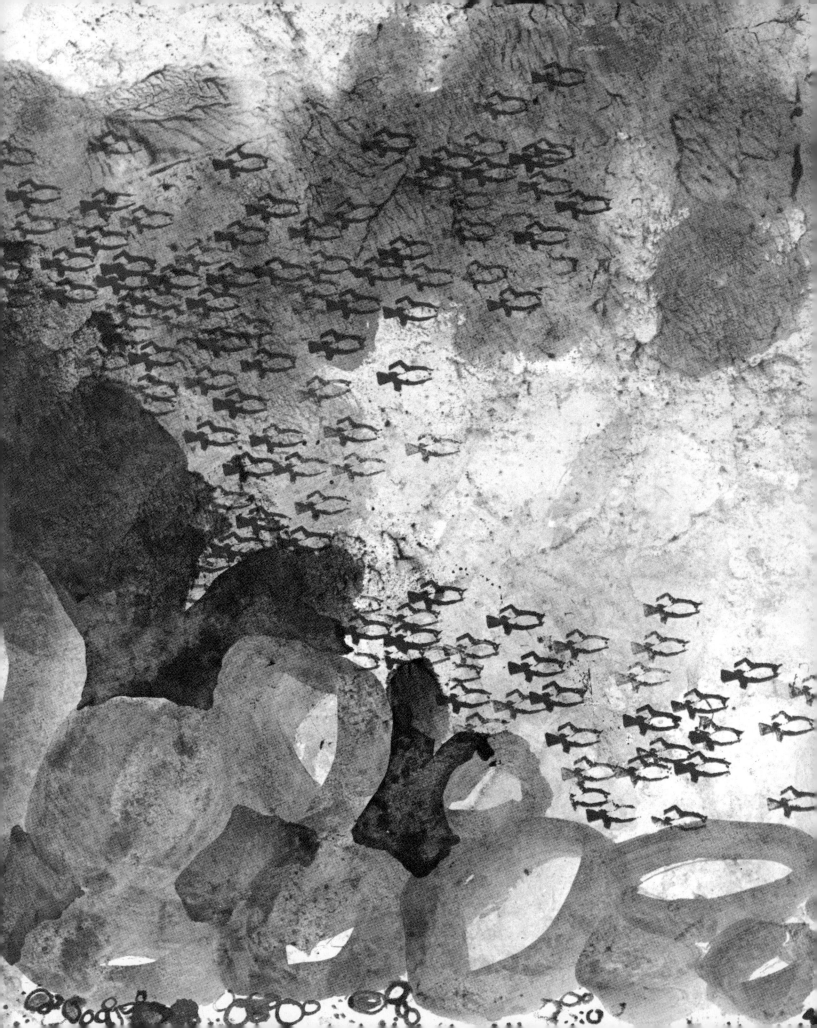

Swimmy thought and thought and thought.

Then suddenly he said, "I have it!"
"We are going to swim all together like the biggest fish in the sea!"

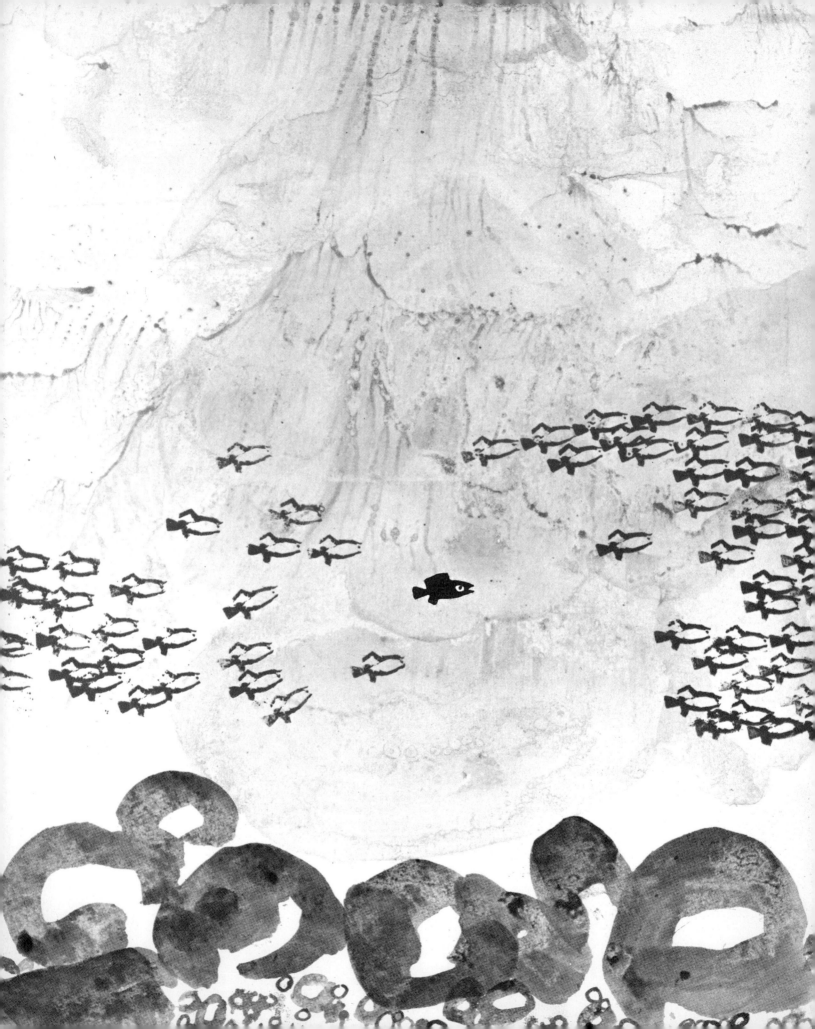

He taught them to swim close together, each in his own place,

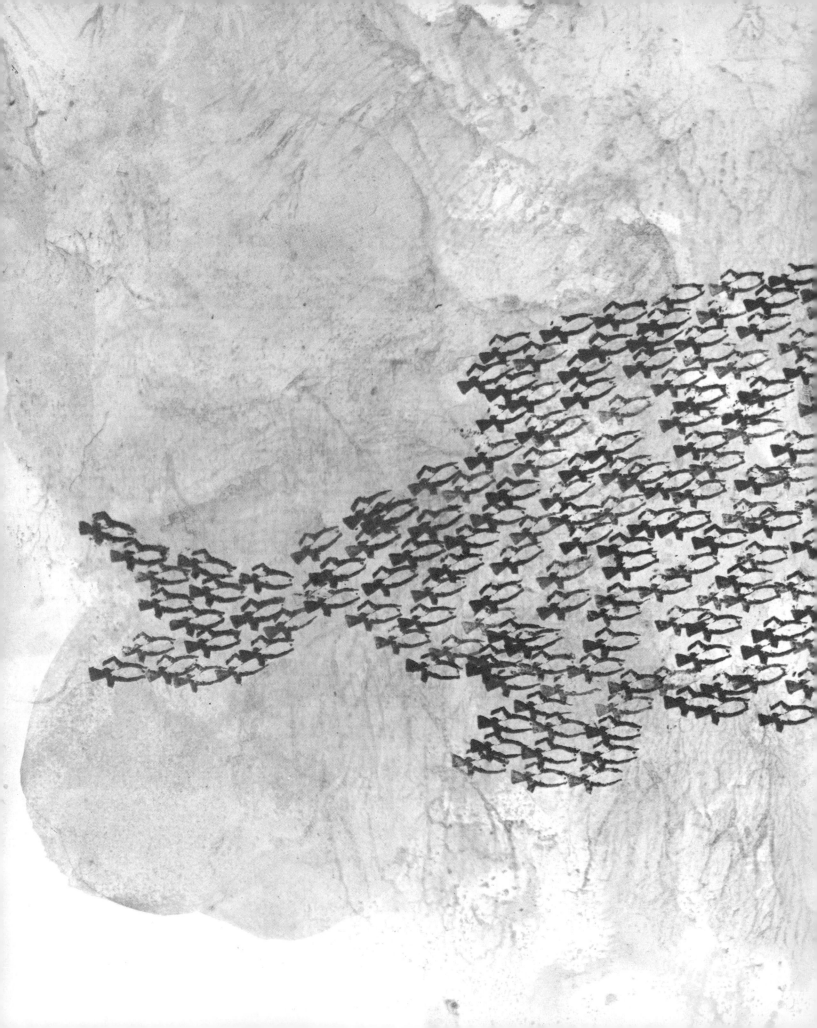

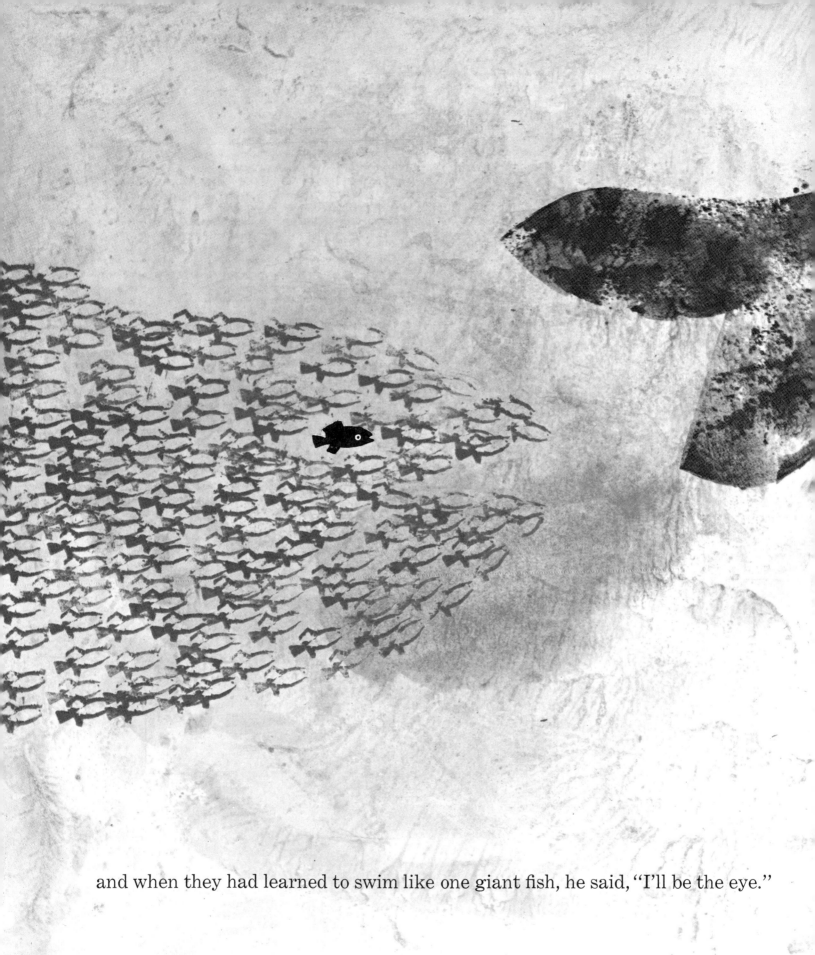

and when they had learned to swim like one giant fish, he said, "I'll be the eye."

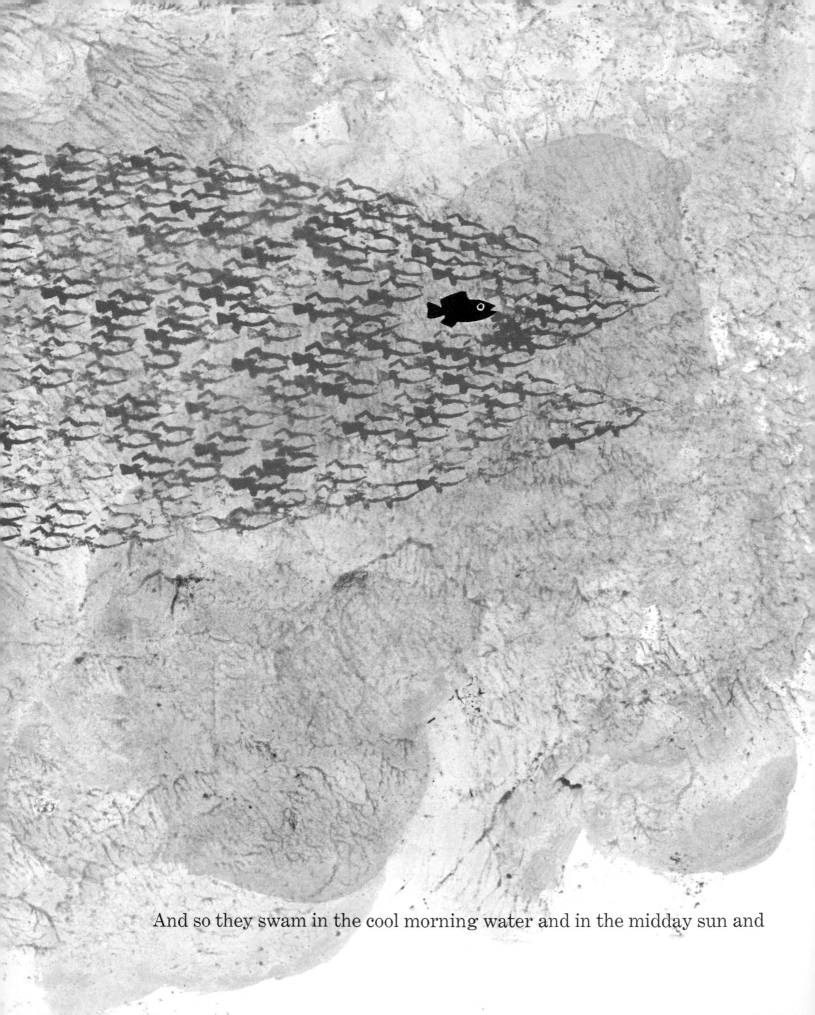

And so they swam in the cool morning water and in the midday sun and

chased the big fish away.

THIS IS A BORZOI BOOK PUBLISHED BY ALFRED A. KNOPF

Copyright © 1963 by Leo Lionni

Copyright renewed 1991 by Leo Lionni

All rights reserved under International and Pan-American Copyright Conventions. Published in the United States of America by Alfred A. Knopf, a division of Random House, Inc., New York, and simultaneously in Canada by Random House of Canada Limited, Toronto. Distributed by Random House, Inc., New York. Originally published by Pantheon Books, a division of Random House, Inc., in 1963.

http://www.randomhouse.com/

Library of Congress Cataloging-in-Publication Data

Lionni, Leo, 1910– . / Swimmy.

p. cm.

ISBN 0-394-81713-3 (trade) — ISBN 0-394-91713-8 (lib. bdg.)

63-8504

Printed in the USA   23   24   25